Published in the UK by
The Bible Reading Fellowship
First Floor, Elsfield Hall, 15-17 Elsfield Way, Oxford OX2 8FG
ISBN 1 84101 423 0

First edition 2005

Copyright © 2005 AD Publishing Services Ltd
1 Churchgates, The Wilderness, Berkhamsted, Herts HP4 2UB
Text copyright © 2005 AD Publishing Services Ltd, Stephanie Jeffs
Illustrations copyright © 2005 Jacqui Thomas

Editorial Director Annette Reynolds
Art Director Gerald Rogers
Pre-production Krystyna Hewitt
Production John Laister

British Library Cataloguing in Publication Data.
A catalogue record for this book is available from the British Library.

Printed and bound in Singapore

JOSH

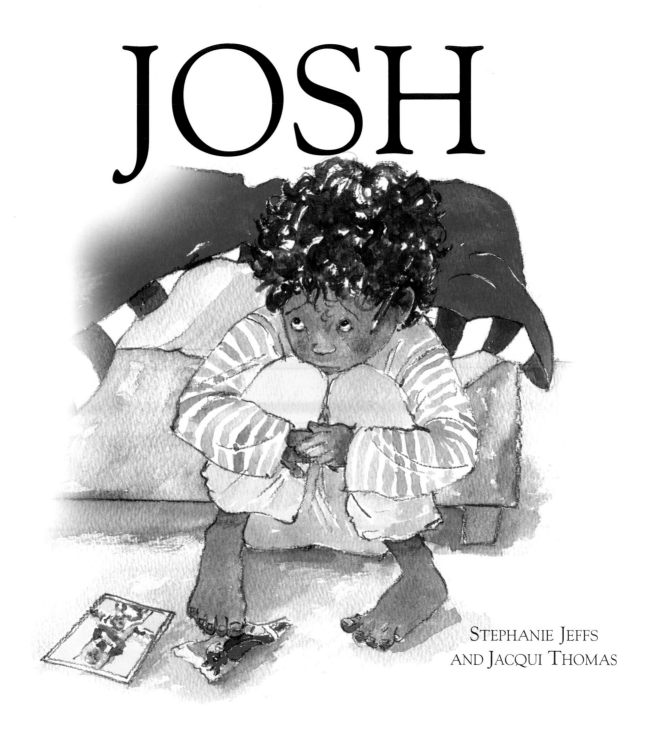

STEPHANIE JEFFS
AND JACQUI THOMAS

Josh and his big sister, Jane, walked past Max's house every day.

Sometimes they saw him through the window. Max always waved.

Sometimes they saw him working in the garden. He loved gardening. In the summer he often gave Josh and Jane an apple from his tree.

Sometimes they saw him pushing his baby daughter on the swing, or playing with his dog.

Max always smiled and waved and said, 'Hello!'

Last year, Mum had asked Max to come and decorate Josh's bedroom.

They had chosen the yellow paint together. They had looked at different picture friezes, until at last they had chosen the paper with bright parrots all around it.

When it was finished, Max thought the room looked brilliant. Josh thought so too.

Mum had taken a photograph of Max and Josh, standing by the ladder.

Sometimes Josh pretended he was Max. He put a pencil behind his ear and tried to whistle.

Josh wanted to be just like Max when he grew up.

11

Sometimes, Josh and Jane would see Max load his ladders and paint brushes on to his van. Josh liked to see the van, with its big sign on the side.

'Cheerio!' called Max, as he drove away from his house.

The children waved. They didn't know anyone else who said, 'Cheerio!' They didn't know anyone else like Max. They liked him very much.

But one day Josh and Jane walked past Max's house and they did not see him.

They couldn't see him through the window, and they couldn't see him in the garden. His van wasn't parked outside his house, and the apples lay on the ground.

'Where's Max?' asked Josh when he got home. 'Where's Max gone, Mum?'

Josh's mum held his hand.

'Josh,' she said, 'something very sad has happened. Max has been in a road accident. He died early yesterday morning.'

'Oh,' said Josh, and switched on the television.

Later Josh lay on his bed. He didn't want to play. He didn't want to do anything. He let his fingers run over the yellow walls. He felt for the join in the paper, and picked at it, until a little rip appeared. He pulled harder.

'Whatever are you doing, Josh?' said
Mum. 'You'll spoil it!'

Josh just grunted. He felt as if
everything was spoilt already.

Mum gave him a cuddle.

'Why did Max have to die, Mum?' asked Josh. 'I don't want never to see him again.' Fat tears began to trickle down his cheeks.

'None of us wanted this to happen, Josh,' said Mum. 'It's hard for everyone. It's hard for Max's family. It's hard for his friends. It's hard for everyone who knew him.'

'I wish it hadn't happened,' muttered Josh. He brushed away the tears and felt under his pillow, reaching for his old blanket. He hadn't used it for a long time, but now he held it to his cheek and pushed his thumb into his mouth.

'What happens when we die?' Josh whispered. 'Where is Max now?'

'Well,' said Mum slowly, 'Max's body was so hurt that it couldn't work any more, but the things that made Max special – his kindness and friendliness, all the things that made Max who he was, which we call his spirit – have gone to be with God.'

Josh tried again. 'But… where's Max left his body? Where is it now?' he asked.
Mum pulled Josh to his feet.

'Come with me,' she said.

Josh followed Mum into the garden. They stood by the flowerbed and looked at the bare patch of earth where the flowers stood in their jar of water.

'Do you remember when Jane's hamster died?' asked Mum. Josh nodded. He remembered it well.

They had put the little hamster in a small box, and buried him under the earth in the garden. Jane had said a prayer. Later, Jane had made a cross out of lollipop sticks, and had written Hammy on it, and put it over the place where they had buried the box.

'The same things happen when a person dies,' explained Mum. 'Their bodies can't feel anything because they are no longer alive.'

'Will Max's body be in a box?'
asked Josh, still thinking of Hammy.

Mum nodded. 'The box is called a
coffin,' she said. 'It will be buried in a
graveyard or a cemetery, or else cremated and
then the ashes scattered in a special place.'

A gust of wind blew some rose petals
into the air. Josh thought about the ashes.

'Will someone say a prayer?' asked Josh.
'Yes,' said Mum, 'at Max's funeral.'

A few days later, Mum, Josh and Jane watched as a large black car stopped outside Max's house. They saw Max's wife and his family get in. 'Max will be buried today,' said Mum. 'They are going to church, to Max's funeral.' Josh half wanted to go to Max's funeral. Mum had told him that Max's family and friends would sing hymns, say prayers and ask God to look after Max. Josh thought about how he and Max had decorated his bedroom. Suddenly Josh felt very cross. 'I don't want to go!' he said firmly.

25

Later that day, Mum, Josh and Jane walked
slowly to the cemetery. They walked past the
greengrocers and Mum and Jane bought a
bunch of flowers. Josh chose a shiny red
apple.

They saw Max's wife and baby
daughter. They saw his family and
friends. Some of them
were dressed in
black, and some of
them were crying.
Josh looked
away.

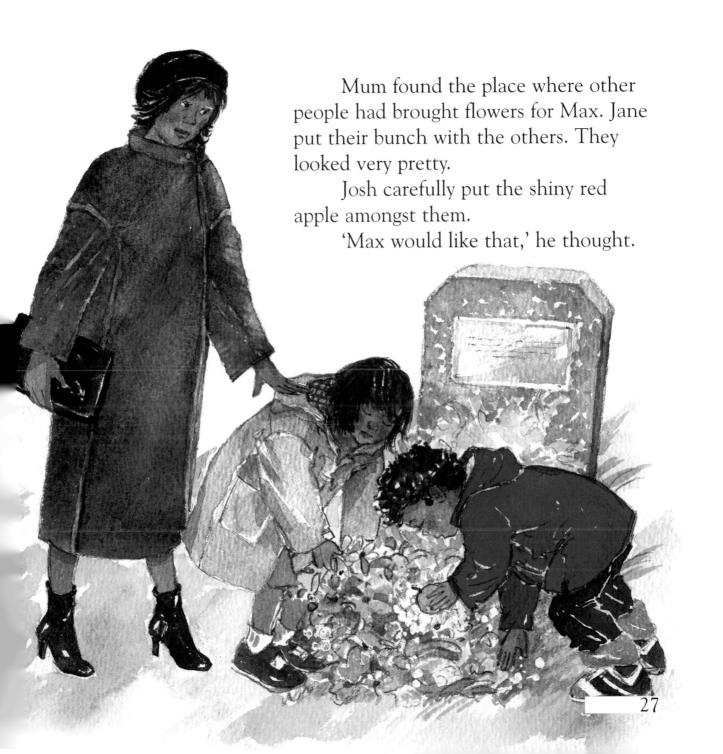

Mum found the place where other people had brought flowers for Max. Jane put their bunch with the others. They looked very pretty.

Josh carefully put the shiny red apple amongst them.

'Max would like that,' he thought.

Later that day, Josh lay in bed. Mum gently stroked his forehead and, after a while, went downstairs.

Josh looked at his yellow walls and the colourful parrots which went around the room.

He got out of bed.

He looked in his drawer and found the photo of Max and himself by the ladder. He found a pencil, and put it behind his ear. He reached under his bed and found a scrap of wallpaper. He arranged them all together on the floor.

Josh sat down beside them and closed his eyes.

'Dear God,' he said, 'thank you for Max. I wish he hadn't died. I will miss him very much. Please look after him in heaven.' Josh opened his eyes. He knew that he would always remember Max. He thought about the swing and the apple tree.

Suddenly, Josh felt a lump in his throat and tears sprang up and ran down his cheeks. Alone in his bedroom, it felt good to cry.